VANNA
KARENINA

ALSO BY FRANK GANNON:

Yo, Poe

FRANK GANNON

VANNA KARENINA

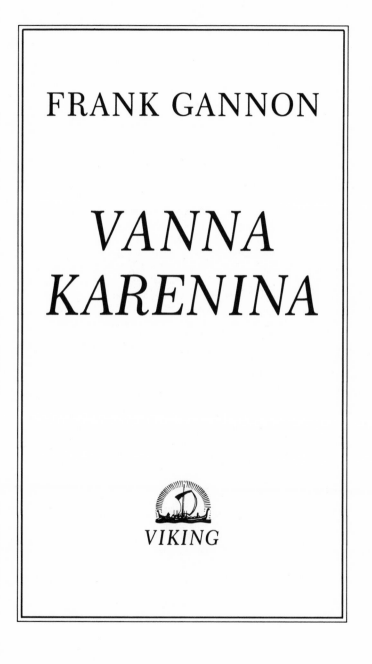

VIKING

VIKING
Published by the Penguin Group
Viking Penguin Inc., 40 West 23rd Street,
New York, New York 10010, U.S.A.
Penguin Books Ltd, 27 Wrights Lane,
London W8 5TZ, England
Penguin Books Australia Ltd, Ringwood,
Victoria, Australia
Penguin Books Canada Ltd, 2801 John Street,
Markham, Ontario, Canada L3R 1B4
Penguin Books (N.Z.) Ltd, 182–190 Wairau Road,
Auckland 10, New Zealand

Penguin Books Ltd, Registered Offices:
Harmondsworth, Middlesex, England

First published in 1988 by Viking Penguin Inc.
Published simultaneously in Canada

1 3 5 7 9 10 8 6 4 2

"Another Fine Mess" (originally titled "That Ollie Summer") and "Of
Dawg and Man" first appeared in *Atlanta*; "Flowers of Evil" and
"Vanna Karenina" in *The Atlantic*; "Bret, Like, Brainstorms" in
Harper's; and "What's Y'all's Sign?" in *Southern*.
Illustrations by Greg King originally appeared with "What's Y'all's
Sign?" in *Southern* and are reproduced by arrangement with
the artist. © Greg King, 1987.
Excerpt from "Sugar, Sugar" by Andy Kim and Jeff Barry. © 1969
Don Kirshner Music Inc. and SBK Blackwood Music Inc. All rights
controlled and administered by SBK Blackwood Music Inc. All rights
reserved. International copyright secured. Used by permission.

LIBRARY OF CONGRESS CATALOGING IN PUBLICATION DATA
Gannon, Frank.
Vanna Karenina.
I. Title.
PN6162.G3   1988   814'.54   87-40630
ISBN 0-670-82080-6

Printed in the United States of America by
Arcata Graphics, Fairfield, Pennsylvania
Set in Primer

*For Aimee, Anne
and Frank, Jr.*

I'd like to thank Gerry Howard, Kris Dahl, Chris Wohl-wend, Jack Hitt, Michael Pollan and Mike Curtis. I'd also like to thank the government of the United States of America.

CONTENTS

Contents

ART SCHOOL
YEARS

> Deals are my art form.
>
> —DONALD TRUMP

No ONE IN MY FAMILY had ever attended college. No wonder I was nervous. I still remember that day my family piled in the car and drove me to the Meadowlands. My knees were knocking. Mom and Dad sat in the front seat and tried to act calm. They talked about the weather and tried to be casual, but I knew that they were very tense, too.

I had always wanted to be an artist. Now it was my chance to find out.

I was headed for the Donald Trump Art School. The name alone intimidated me. Yet here I was, going off for my freshman year. It all seemed so strange. I had never dreamed of being accepted, let alone getting a full scholarship for four years. It was beyond my wildest dreams.

I remember my first sight of the place, when my parents pulled up in front.

"Gosh," said my father, "this place just knocks the crap out of me."

"This guy Trump must be loaded," said my mother.

I remember saying good-bye to my parents, kissing them good-bye and calling a redcap to get my stuff. I guess everybody has college memories like that, but even now I

3

get a little choked up when I think of my first day in school.

I still remember getting to my room, tipping the guy, turning on the tube and lying down on the bed to eat the little mint they had on the pillow and reading the catalogue. Yes, I thought, it was going to be tough.

BACHELOR OF FINE ARTS DEGREE REQUIREMENTS

Students may pursue this program through a concentration in one of ten areas: Big Deals, Soft Cons, Bum Deals, Ripoffs, Screw-jobs, Bust-out Games, Carney Stuff, Sucker Raps, Flatty Gimmicks, and Razzle-Dazzle Marble Games.

Studio Major (210 credit hours)

		QUARTER HOURS
I	Humanities	20
II	Mathematics and Natural Science	20
III	Social Science	20
IV	Deal Foundations	45
	The Toteboard I	
	The Toteboard II	
	Skill vs. Chance	
	The Historical Background of Deals	
	Nickles and Dimes	
	Mister Minus	
	Protection Money	
	Adding I	
	Subtraction I	
	Adding II	
	Subtraction II	
	Protection Money II	

Portfolio Review—Application to the Major

V	Major Concentration	85
	Deal Theory	5–15
	Studio	70–80

Second Portfolio Review—Bust-out Time

VI	Money Changes Hands	20

TOTAL   210

I was a little bit taken aback. No cheap degree here, I thought. Work, work, work.

Things were so much different from high school! Everybody was so intense, and I was always worried that I'd miss something important. You never wanted to stop concentrating. If you did stop concentrating, even for a minute in the hall, say, or the Ratskeller, there are always the likelihood that you would either fall behind in school or get made as a mark by two guys from Miami Beach and get your bankbook worked over big time.

After a while, though, I got used to it. I sat in front of the mirror for hours at a time practicing. After a while I got very good. One night, late at night in a nightclub with the dean, I said to him, "Dean Rhinhart, let's toss for my tuition. Double or nothing. Call it in the air."

What Rhinhart didn't know was that I was using a jobbed coin, two tails. Rhinhart said, "Let's go for it." I flipped.

"Tails," he called.

I caught the coin and put it away in my pocket.

"Just wanted to see if you had any sporting blood, Dean," I said and smiled at him.

He bought it.

I was a freshman then. When I think back on those days I find myself smiling privately to myself. How jejune can one guy get?

I remember my first day in Madame Gozabill's class. I was very nervous because of Madame Gozabill's reputation as a hard marker. Even before our first class day she had distributed copies of her reading list and it was absolutely brutal: KNOW YOUR STARS, KING TUT, GYPSY NOSTRILS, ULYSSES. Absolutely brutal stuff.

One day in class, toward the end of the quarter, I happened to mention that I had had a dream. Madame Gozabill asked me all the details of my dream, told me to wear plaid slacks and sell my home. I thought she was joking around and I laughed. I got a *D* and I was lucky.

I was thinking about transferring, but things got better. Things got a lot better. I met a broad-tossing mob in my sophomore year, and I began, slowly at first, to see myself as an artist, or at least someone who would be spending his life involved with art.

I remember looking out my dorm window and seeing the same parking lot I always saw. But on that July morning so long ago, I remember seeing something else, something that signaled to me that art wasn't something remote, something to be stashed away in some private collection and eventually given to a museum. No, art was something that you breathed in order to live. Art was something you drank in order to not be thirsty.

I saw, out there on that parking lot, a green 1966 Mustang with a FOR SALE sign and a number, and I got that dude for pocket change. Then I turned around and sold it big time.

Life began.

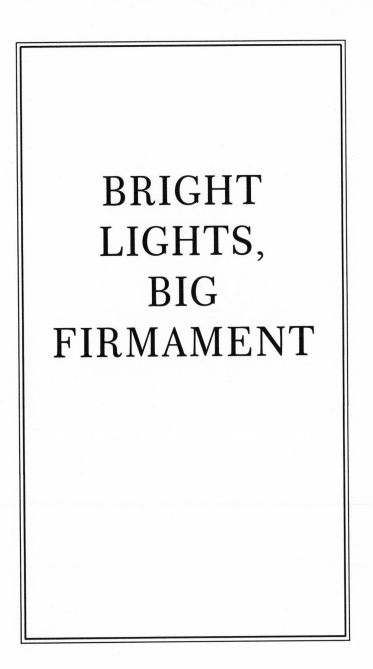

BRIGHT
LIGHTS,
BIG
FIRMAMENT

WHAT HE TELLS YOU is that the earth is without form. You notice that he has a plan and his facial gestures give him away. He wants to call the light *day* and the dark *night*. You look at him and you can see him thinking behind that big white beard. And you think, there's this big guy who is all powerful, but he's just a guy like you. And you start to think of all this and then you say to yourself, *What a guy*. You want to watch this guy and see what he does. And he tells you that he wants to call the firmament *heaven* and he wants the water *seas*, and you find yourself thinking about what is going on with this guy.

Still, you are not quite sure of this big guy and you think that if you could just get to the bathroom and *bring forth* some extreme nose unction you might be able to see what he means when he's talking about herb yielding seed and fruit yielding fruit and whatever else he's going on about. You can't be quite sure at this point because it is very noisy in there and this big guy is talking like New Jersey in a wind tunnel. But you know that you better not do any more nose unction because you can still taste the last nose unction on the back of your tongue and you realize that it is still the first day.

11

A little later you will see what is at work here. It is a jungle motif. You take a look around—great whales, winged fowl, some ferns, everything that creepeth—and you wonder how you got here.

It was your friend, "King" James, of course. He brought you here, crammed a vial in your shirt pocket and left. James. What a guy he was, always worried that someone, somewhere, might be having a slightly better time. He was like a cockroach on acid, he couldn't take a break. He just dove head first into life with all his clothes on. James actually believed in witches and black magic. He actually wrote, at one time, a book all about it called *Demonology*. William Shakespeare wrote Macbeth to try to get in good with James, and it worked. Now Shakespeare was one of the people James called. James was either very, very smart or very, very dumb. You could never figure out which. James's circle of acquaintance ran the gamut from high-brow to not even close to having a brow. What a group they were: that chick who looked over at you last week and told you, very softly, that you pronounced the word *consummate* wrong. Ben Jonson. The Earl of Man. Viscount Falkland. All those women with all those cheek-bones. They were all so shallow. Yet you found something attractive about them, didn't you?

You go out and walk in the blazing sunshine and your tongue burns and you start to murmur and curseth and you almost bump into a guy and he curseth you.

•   •   •

There's this woman you work with, Sarah. She's the West Village, I-can-handle-it type. She's older than you are but you can't tell how much older. She's easy to talk to and she laughs nice and she's still very pretty. You've met her husband, Abraham, who is a lot older. Abraham is an anal retentive, up front, East Side guy who neglects his wife.

You should call Sarah. You make a mental note about this but then you realize that you've made way too many mental notes. They might as well be *The Notes to and from the Underground.*

What a guy you are. You're really something, aren't you?

You go home.

Your doorman buzzes and you go over and answer it. It turns out to be King James.

"Hey, you got any demons up there?" he asks.

"No."

"I'm coming up."

You and King James do a lot of lines and hit every bar you see.

Finally you're walking back with two beers in this little club where they have stuffed animals glued to the walls and you feel this tap on your shoulder and you turn around and it's Goliath.

You haven't seen him in five years. Goliath's a pro jock. Big money, but he knows he's over the hill now. You look at him and you see he's still basking in the glow of the glory days. He was in your dining club in college and he still looks the same. He asks you how you're doing and you lie. You ask him what he's doing and he says that he's just hanging around.

"I was over in Babylon," he says, leaning over and hollering into your ear, which bothers you because there's nobody else in the bar and it's completely quiet in there. "Didn't I hear that you married a Nubian?"

"No, I married a handmaiden, but she left me about a year ago. Last I heard somebody saw her with an Assyrian on Houston Street."

Goliath acts like he can't leave you fast enough and he does.

You wake up today and you say, to hell with everything. Today I'm going to *write*.

You always wanted to be a writer but your time was always taken up with so many little unimportant details. Often you found, when you came back from a night of two hundred bars and countless lines, there was absolutely no time for what you wanted to do most: write.

Now you would take the time. You get out your Sears Scholar typewriter, crank up the paper and get ready.

Suddenly you hear a very loud noise out in the street. You run to your window and look out. No writing tonight. It's the Apocalypse out there. Four Horsemen. Seven seals. The whole bit.

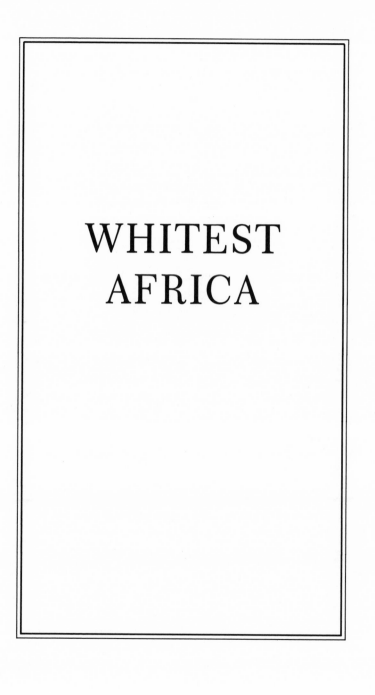

WHITEST
AFRICA

HERE I AM AGAIN, after all these years, twenty-five or thirty of them, taking pen in hand to tell you of what it was like when I was young and lived in Africa. Although it has been so long, I can still see myself there, still close my eyes and see the way that it was: the wind whipping across the plain, the rows of hunters going in front of me to comb the brush, the stars twinkling in that darkest of skies that is Africa's.

All of these things are there for me when I shut my eyes.

When I was a child I spent my days with the Kakewpie, hunting naked in the bush or in the rain forests of the Galstosee. We would hunt all day and then I would return home and my mother would make me a big bowl of Campbell's Country Vegetable Soup.

When I was a child I hunted all the time. At first I had a hard time hunting the swift capped langur and the cunning red-capped mangabey, but my friends among the Kakewpie were very kind and patient with me. I remember the first day I went hunting with them. Nobody had told me that we were all going to be naked, and I showed up in absolutely the worst thing: a midnight rose silk tee,

17

cotton/polyester Lycra spandex shorts and some Reeboks. I looked around at everybody else and I could have died. But the Kakewpie, all naked and smiling, didn't even laugh at me. They were *too* kind, those Kakewpie, if that's possible.

"Why do you dress like that?" one Kakewpie asked. "Your head is filled with dawn-fog today, is that it?"

Maybe my head was filled with dawn-fog that day, but I was young and I soon learned. Lycra spandex was for holy days, not hunting days.

There were so many things to hunt: muntjac, chousingha, ibex, dik-dik, gayal, bushback, ree-ja-mo, klipspringer, cerothere, bharal, chevrotain, oryx, blesbok, eland, geese, ducks, cows. There were so many things to hunt. There were even some big furry-looking things, but I don't know what they were.

And there was Thompson's gazelle. And sometimes Thompson, but usually only on weekends.

And, after a long day of hunting all of these things, Dad would drive me home in the wagon with all of the bumper stickers. And I'd try to get a rock-format station on the radio.

When Dad picked me up I'd wave good-bye and call out to my Kakewpie friends out the window.

I'd wave like crazy.

"Good-bye, Karkoweel!"

"Good-bye, Kokobeaner!"

And they'd call back.

"Good-bye, Dawn-fog head!"

"Good-bye, Skill-ball head!"

After a day like that, I'd always fall asleep in front of the TV, no matter what was on.

There was a place called Mustachandbeard, and I used to ride to it on horseback or sometimes Dad would let me take the Plymouth Horizon. And there was an old man there whom I got very close to on several occasions. He would tell me about the Gogowiplash and the Mojomen, and the great leaders of the past and the great priests and magicians that had once lived there. He would tell me about Mount Moonyou and the mountain of beasts, Lizardlandthemepark.

I would sit for hours listening to the old man and his stories of how things had been before they put up the mall. And later, when I returned to my home and family, I would find myself sitting quietly and thinking while I watched a couple videos of what the old man had said.

One day the old man and I were out at Mustachandbeard watching some cape buffalo rut. The old man turned to me, and I guess I'll always remember what he said.

"Cape buffalo are better than most men. They rut better, for instance."

He was a very wise old man.

Finally, I remember leaving Africa. I got out of the taxi at the airport, and the wise old man, who was riding with me, helped me with my luggage. I looked around me. To the west I saw the Notmysister Hills, their majestic peaks seeming to support the very sky. To the east I saw the awesome sight of Mount Liquidpaper. It was so far away that I couldn't remember how big it really was. It was like a still, blue cloud, or something. Like my memories of Africa.

Then I thought, crap, I forgot my hair dryer.

ANOTHER
FINE MESS

I USED TO THINK that I knew the key. I needed to be an individual, one man. Then something bad would happen to me or, more than likely, to somebody I was allegedly related to or involved with in some way. Then I would shoulder roll into action. I would know exactly what to do.

Now things are different. I guess it started when Sylvester Stallone's *Cobra* came out last year and it didn't really do that well. That was supposed to be a *Cobra* summer. It shook me. It was summer. It was very hot. Yet it was not a *Cobra* summer.

My nephew was the first to notice when I came into the house with a big box full of sunglasses, shoulder holsters and kitchen matches.

"Sorry, Uncle," he said. "Haven't you seen the papers? It's not going to be a *Cobra* summer. It's going to be some other kind of summer."

I sat and read the papers with a kitchen match in my mouth. I was stunned, but there could no doubt: This, the summer of '86, was not going to be a *Cobra* summer.

I was crushed, but what could I do? I waited silently for about ten months.

Now comes this summer. Nobody tells me anything,

and I'm paying attention *all* the time. I don't know what to do. Is this a Gilbert and Sullivan summer, for crissakes? Somebody help me out here.

Then I found out. It was an Ollie North summer.

First I went to the barber and asked him for an Ollie. He didn't know what I meant, so I showed him a picture. He gave me a good one, even got the cowlick right.

Then I was out on the street. Out in the Ollie North summer. First I walked past a storefront and noticed what I was wearing: gray, elastic-waist shorts, tube socks, white sneakers and a Cat Diesel T-shirt. All wrong. I dug through my wallet for my credit cards; then I got busy. It wasn't really that hard and, by that afternoon, I was almost completely into the Ollie summer thing. I got a nice green army coat at I. Goldberg. I got the shirt and tie at Liquidation Mart. The hardest part was finding the medals. I got the ribbons OK, but I had to settle for plastic medals. One of them had HE MAN on it, but I don't think anybody noticed.

I went home and practiced talking into a mirror. By that evening I pretty much had it down. "That sounds like a really neat idea," I said, and I sounded almost just like Jimmy Stewart.

Once I was satisfied with the voice, I had to work on my behavior patterns, which really needed work. I'd get up early, make coffee and read the ball scores, just like always, but afterward, I'd go out in the backyard and shred the sports section. I didn't have a real shredder, so I used my rake.

Also, I decided to change a lot of my ways at work. I

used to have a little problem with authority, but, at least for the summer, if anybody that I even *suspected* of being my superior asked me to do anything, I'd do it without a second thought. Once, about the beginning of July, this guy I used to see in the hall told me to go over to the corner and stand on my head, and that's just what I did. And I stayed on my head until I was told otherwise. I remember staying overnight on my head many times that summer, and I'd do it again.

Still, something was missing from my Ollie summer. I decided to divert some funds. I went over to the sofa and took out the cushions. I got like three or four dollars in change out of there. Then I took the change and threw it out into the yard. Almost immediately I felt a lot better.

I started making my wife stand behind me a lot. At first she didn't like it. Once she started screaming. After a while, though, she realized what was going on, and she went along with it. She was always standing behind me. In grocery stores. Waiting for a bus. I didn't have to turn around because I knew she was back there. I could feel her hot breath on the back of my neck.

She's my best friend.

Soon, before I knew it, it was nearly the end of August. I put away my uniform and I grew a mustache. I stopped diverting funds. I watched the sun go down earlier and earlier and I felt that first chill wind of autumn. I knew that it was over now, but I'll always remember fondly the summer of '87: that Ollie summer, a time of magic.

HE LIKED
THE WAY
SHE FORMED
HER
SENTENCES

RICK COTTA STRODE PURPOSEFULLY into the lobby of the best hotel in the world and everybody was just a gawkin at him. He had power, money, good clothes and perfect teeth. He was some special. He'd jest about make your teeth fall out and you'd get tore up if you looked at him too longly.

He were just about the best damn thing that weuns had ever set eyes on. He was some stuff. He was a tuna. Mamaanem said that they'da liked to clamp onto Rick Cotta and jess pray for lockjaw.

"Hey, Rick, you all gittin any strange," cooed a sultry young seductress who was jest a settin at the bar.

Rick Cotta jest started a grinnin to beat all. He knowed that when he smiled like that the fat lady was ready to start a singin. Nobody could resist Rick Cotta and that smile. To try to resist that was like a bug a arguin with a chicken.

"Ain't changed my oil in nigh on a week," said Rick Cotta as he strode purposefully into the Polo Lounge.

She sat gawkin at the backside of Rick Cotta and she comenced to praying for lockjaw.

29

Rick Cotta just sashayed into the Polo Lounge and jest parked his butt in the best damn seat they had in that godforsaken dump. He sat down next to this person who was already settin there. Rick Cotta knowed this person so it wasn't no big problem or nothing like that.

This boy that Rick Cotta was a knowin was sorry. He was just about the sorriest boy that Rick Cotta knowed and he knowed some of the sorriest boys that they had them there at that there Polo Loungue. Yeah, that Howie, he was about as sorry a boy as Rick Cotta had ever had the misfortune of bein accused of squintin at.

"Hey Rick Cotta, boy," said Howie, "you gettin any strange?"

"Your sorry," said Rick Cotta. He motioned the waitress over and she slud right over and it looked to me that she was comencing to start in praying for lockjaw.

"Fetch me some of them there Profiteroles Variées and some of that there Salade d'Oeufs à la Russe. Now git."

"I'll git," said the waitress, who was just a grinnin, "but first I have to know what-all you goin ta be drinkin."

Rick Cotta jest gave her that look that said "Whatever-you'd-be-havin-darlin-is-the-thing-that-I-will-be-havin-sweetcakes." He was very good at that look. He was thirty-seven and he just about beat all.

And don't you know that she just went right over and fetched Rick Cotta a big old glass of Perrier. And she jest slapped that thing right down there on the table in front of Rick Cotta. And old Rick Cotta, he looked like he was actin good for a change.

This boy Howie was the head of Paramount Pictures.

He was like some kind of bigshot. But he was still sorrier than all getout. He was settin there jest a grinnin at old Rick Cotta.

Rick Cotta took a little taste of his Salade d'Oeufs à la Russe. He smiled over at Howie.

"What are you a gawkin at?" he asked calmly.

"That heffer over there. You ever saw anything like that?"

Rick Cotta turned around and saw the most beautiful damn woman in the history of the world. She was five foot eleven inches tall. Her neck was swan-like. The curves of her body belied him slimness. The greenness of her eyes was bedazzling. Her nostrils flared upward until they flirted with and became involved with her cheekbones. Rick Cotta, as sophisticated as he was, found himself a prayin for lockjaw.

"Let me ask you something, in all confidence." Rick Cotta leaned forward to talk in confidence to with Howie, who was still as sorry as they come. "Are you knowin that?"

Howie jest leaned back and started in a snortin and chuckin.

"Yeah. I reckon I knows her, she's my damn sister."

The sex was good but not great.

FLOWERS OF EVIL: ASK CHARLES BAUDELAIRE

Q: *What annuals are suitable for planting near the ocean?*

If sufficient depth of topsoil (seven to nine inches) is provided and you give them sufficient water in dry periods (which drag on and on, furrowing into your soul, often), you should be in pretty good shape to grow almost any annual that strikes your fancy. A tip: don't get hopelessly drunk before you start, and don't approach the project through the miasma of despair. Also, remember the gloves and stay busy.

Q: *The crowns of my veronicas are rising above the surface. Can I do anything about this?*

Veronicas tend to raise their crowns if they're kept in the same spot too long. They've been stagnant and they're starting to fester; like madmen in the dark, with great wild eyes they are coming to get you, because your corrupted hand should never touch beauty.

If your heart is set on it, move the veronicas in a large soil bag. Then return to your life of error and sin, until you, too, die and fester in a very large soil bag.

Q: *Is it all right to trim trees in the winter?*
Yes, provided the temperature isn't too low. Also, check
the trees. If black regiments of larvae flow out of the trees
like a dense, ghastly river, and the stench of death is over-
powering, throw the trees away; it's way past trimming
time. But bear in mind that you, too, will turn into a rotting
mass, to be eaten by vermin. My love!

Q: *Which trees and shrubs are suitable for sandy soil in*
a sunny location?
With proper care, arcadia and tamarisk should do well.
Since half of horticulture is visual, you might think about
putting one or two vile, rotting corpses, their legs in the
air like lustful women's, out there somewhere. Use your
own judgment, but I'd give the amount of shade more
than a second thought for the corpses. Remember to
mulch.

Q: *How can I make a medium-size, manure-heated hotbed*
to get an early start on tomatoes?
Find some long two-by-fours and make a box. The size is
up to you, but make sure that it's square. If you can make
it voluptuous that's a plus. Make it ripe. Make it trium-
phant! Make it corrupt, rich, voluptuous, rich, and trium-
phant! Make it strange and untamed and then wet it with
your tears of anguish.

Grow your tomatoes earlier than others, and sing of their
round red beauty. Sing of your depraved globes and know
that they are your brothers! Brothers of pestilence! Oh,
your mind and your early tomatoes spring from the very

same vine! Use a 2-10-10 general fertilizer—unless you can live comfortably with the idea that you might need more potash.

Q: *Should tulip bulbs be taken up each year and separated? Should they be covered with leaves in the fall?*
It really depends on where you live. If you live in the Midwest, then I'd leave them where they are for two or three years, unless you're going to use the land for something else—like maybe a few naked black rocks over which flow a great deal of personal humiliation, until you lie palsied in your loins.

That's probably a long-term project. Forget the leaves, too. You probably have too much time on your hands, if you're asking questions like that.

Q: *Which plants, besides geraniums, can be grown in a small home greenhouse for winter bloom?*
When you set out your plants, you will find that a lot of flowers you wouldn't think of can produce winter blooms. But be careful. Studies at Cornell University indicate that if you're like other amateur gardeners, you'll probably wind up staring straight into the grim, still face of death. Go to your greenhouse without love or remorse, amateur gardener. Debud your chrysanthemums in sin!

Seriously, I'm always eager to help the amateur horticulturalist, because I know his ambitions and his many problems.

As always, yours for good gardening and hideous suffering.

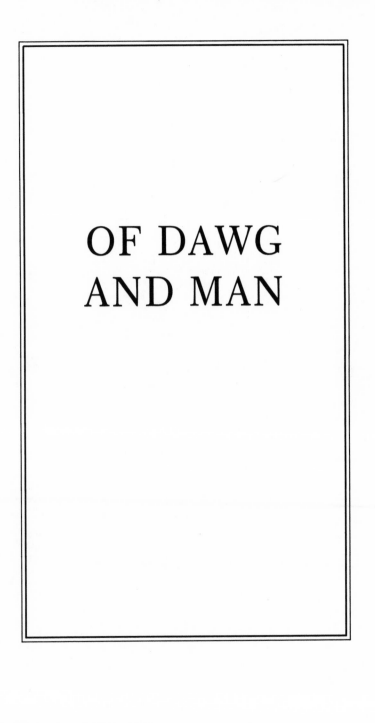

OF DAWG
AND MAN

WE ARE MOVING into a sensitive area here. This is the area where one wakes up on Sunday morning with a feeling of humiliation deep in the pit of one's stomach as slowly, almost imperceptibly, the memories of Saturday make their way up the ladder to your consciousness.

Why? Why did you feel that you had to get down on your knees and make growling and barking noises in front of your friends and acquaintances? What did you have in mind?

If there is comfort in numbers, you may take that comfort. Dylan Thomas, for one. In Paul Ferris's autobiography of Thomas we learn how Thomas actually broke a tooth doing his dog impersonation. Thomas, of course, also wrote *Portrait of the Artist as a Young Dawg* (sic). Some of his little-known poetry clearly shows the Welsh bard as an avatar of many of those who now dwell between the hedges.

> Though lovers be lost love shall not;
> And death shall have no dominion.
> Hunker down!

41

Acting like a dog obviously leaves considerable scars on the psyche, yet the phenomenon persists. Perhaps it is just another manifestation of man's continuing search for meaning, a quest that can take many forms: meditation, organized religion, philosophy, drinking a quart of Jim Beam, dressing in a giant black hat, barking, growling.

Perhaps it is best to study the phenomenon from the outside, from the observer's perspective. It's probably a good idea not to ask anyone who barks. More than you have to, anyway.

Aimee is fifteen years old. She doesn't even understand the rules of football. She has seen only one football game in her life: the Georgia-Vandy game last fall. Hers is the "Beginner's Mind" much sought after by devotees of Eastern religion. Through her we can see what's going on here.

"We got there and it was very pretty. The sun was shining and it was really crowded. I had to sit with the older people and I was sitting near this lady who had this crazy silver dress on. It was like a metallic dress, really short, and I looked over at the lady and she must have been like fifty years old. Then it was time for the kickoff and all of these people around me started to make all these funny sounds. At first I didn't know what it was, but then I realized that they were all growling, and pretty soon someone would start barking or howling. It went on like that almost the whole game. There was always somebody howling or barking or growling.

"Next time I want to sit with the students."

Now let us hear from the mouth of the Dawg itself. J.B.,

thirty-nine, is a restaurant manager. He is the apotheosis of bulldog. On game day he wears red and black, eats fried chicken, and starts drinking while the cartoons are still on.

"I been going since I went to school there. I never finished, and my wife says that's why I keep going back. I've missed maybe two games the last ten years.

"The barking? Yeah, I've done that, some. I don't *plan* to do it. It just happens. That's what's fun about it, I guess.

"They have all these signs all over Sanford Stadium saying that you're not supposed to drink, but everybody does anyway. Right now I've got this little rubber sandwich that's got a flask in it. You're supposed to look like you're eating a sandwich, but you're really drinking.

"It's just for laughs. I bring a bottle, too, for serious drinking. I bring the little rubber sandwich because I've always had a weakness for that James Bond–gadget kind of crap.

"I guess I'll always bark. But I won't plan it."

How deep can Dawg run? Pretty deep, says Oliver Saks, doctor and writer. Saks describes a young man who, one night, dreamt he was a dawg (sic). When the young man awoke, he found that he was still a dawg (sic). How was it? It was great! He could smell emotions! Fear, contentment, happiness—they all had their own separate smell! When he was a dawg (sic), the young man walked through a wonderland of emotional and physical excitement. When he finally returned to normal, it was with a profound sense of loss.

We can all return to that wonderland, at least in the fall. Just be sure to contribute to the alumni fund-raisers, and be sure to buy one of those bulldog clocks. They're attractive *and* functional.

Also, knee pads might be a good idea.

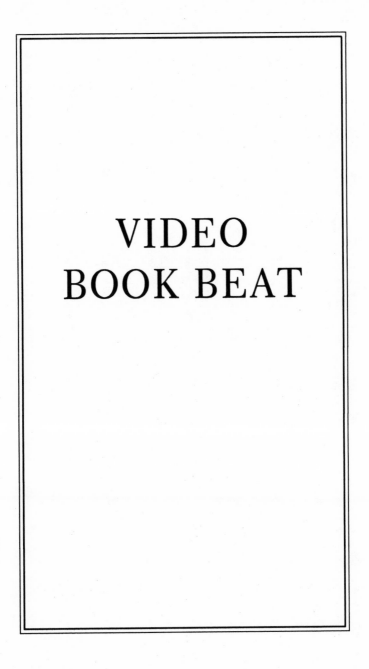

VIDEO
BOOK BEAT

Basing videos on best-selling books is another strategy for promoting sales. The potential of book/video tie-ins is luring publishers into the field.

—*Business Week*

Norman Mailer: *The Naked and the Dead*—The naked and the dead indeed. There's enough of both here to satisfy anybody. With all the smoke bombs and flesh comes a lot more, however, and that's what makes this video such a satisfying grabber. Here, Norman and the boys sit on the island of Anopopei and, with considerable style, show just what a great novel is all about. It's just a handful of exhausted men faced with an impossible and futile mission on an unprotected invasion beach, but, hey, it doesn't really matter: they all play their asses off. Mailer's laid-back, pop-influenced sentences are a joy. The close-ups of his nostril hairs are a delight. By the end of the video nobody really cares if anybody comes back alive or not. *The Naked and the Dead* is just that and more: it's also great.

William Golding: *The Lord of the Flies*—A more suitable title might have been *Bored with the Flies*. Half of this video is in black and white and the other half is in color. Who cares? This is your basic retrograde heavy metal number; I *love* your boring clichés. Shall I count them? I know you're screaming, "Don't!" but it's my column: atomic war, youths on a beach, screaming fans, a big plane crash, winding guitars, conch shells, flashy stage visuals. Need I go on? Watching a seventyish Golding leaping around on a stage is not my idea of excitement. And the thing with cutting the fake pig's head off and placing it on a pole as an offering to the monster, doesn't this all belong on the "Muppets" show? I'll take Miss Piggy. At least she's cute.

Thomas Pynchon: *Gravity's Rainbow*—Ho-hum. Disorientation time again, and didn't it come *quickly* this time? Pynchon's a nice enough guy—the kind of guy you'd like to sit around and drink ten draft beers with—but haven't we been down this path before? The sweaty Pynchon mugging for the camera, the frantic fans, the famous raised fist gesture that brings the same predictable result as always. Who *cares* about any of this anymore? If I have to look at Pynchon squat down, plug a cord into the socket and get "blown away" by the supposed "overload," I think I'm going to have to sit down and ask myself why I'm doing this for a living in the first place.

Lewis Thomas: *The Lives of a Cell*—Even back in his anemic, pre-dance music era, Lewis has always been more cultist than crossover, and that's still the case. Like Gould or Sagan, Thomas likes to jam on ideas, and he's up to more of the same here. But unlike Gould and Sagan you could never call Lewis artsy. With his dark bass runs and his infectious "Let's pretend that the world is just a big damn cell" dance mix, this is hard stuff to resist. Yet, after three or four looks, you might find yourself thinking, as I did, *If that's all there is to the world, like just one big cell, why should anybody bother?* Thomas doesn't make me physically sick, but neither do a lot of other things.

Saul Bellow: *Humboldt's Gift*—This video looks like one of those MTV-type ads for some form of trendy nonsense. The women all are beautiful, the interiors look like they were done by Bobby Guccione, the men look like they all stepped out of a page from some slick, mindless fashion mag. In other words, the whole thing looks like you could throw it off a building today and come back and catch it next week. But hey, that's all OK because you have to ask yourself, *How many times have I seen a video for a book that was* this *bouncy?* Not many, I bet.

WHAT'S
Y'ALL'S SIGN?

IT HAS BECOME PRETTY OBVIOUS to me that the astrological signs that we have have served their purpose, and we should get rid of them. They're just too *weird* for me. When I'm out driving around I'll see bulls, and once in a great while I suppose I'll even see a ram. Up the street from me there's some twins, but I don't see them much. The rest of these things are just too obscure. You only see crabs on vacation. There's no lions, or scorpions, not many archers and no damn water bearers. Virgins? The neighborhood's not crawling with them either, needless to say.

So what we need here is some relevance. We need things we can recognize up there in the night sky. That's what I'm doing here.

One note about accuracy. These signs are very accurate.

•   •   •

MOON PIE
March 21 through April 20

You are the type that spends a lot of time on the front porch. It's a cinch to recognize the physical appearance of Moon Pies. *Big* and *round* are the key words here.

You should marry anybody that you can get remotely interested in the idea. It's not going to be easy.

This might be the year to think about aerobics. Maybe not.

POSSUM
April 21 through May 21

When confronted with life's difficulties, Possums have a marked tendency to withdraw and develop a "Don't bother me about it" attitude. Sometimes you become so withdrawn people actually think that you are dead. This strategy is probably not psychologically healthy, but it seems to work for you. One day, however, it won't work, and you may find your problems actually running you over.

CRAWFISH
May 22 through June 21

Crawfish is a water sign. If you work in an office, the Crawfish will always be hanging around the water cooler. They prefer the beach to the mountains, the pool to the golf course, the bathtub to the living room.

Crawfish tend to be not particularly attractive physically, but they have very, very good heads.

COLLARDS
June 22–July 23

Collards have a genius for communication. They love to get in the "melting pot" of life and share their essence with the essence of those around them.

Collards make good social workers, psychologists and baseball managers.

As far as your personal life goes, if you are Collards, stay away from Moon Pies. It just won't work. Save yourself a lot of heartache.

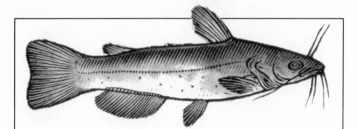

CATFISH
July 24 through August 23

"One does not invite a Catfish to dinner with a Crawfish," jokes southern astrologer Roderick "Bo" Fusco. "Too many bones."

Jokes aside, Catfish are traditionalists in matters of the heart, although note: whiskers may cause problems for loved ones.

Seriously, Catfish are never easy people to understand. They prefer the muddy bottoms to the clear surfaces of life.

Above all else, Catfish should stay away from Moon Pies.

GRITS

August 24 through September 23

Your highest aim is to be with others like yourself. You like to huddle together with a big crowd of other Grits. You love to travel, though, so maybe you should think about joining a club. Where do you like to go? Anywhere. Anywhere they have cheese or gravy or bacon or butter or eggs. If you can go somewhere where they have all these things, you are very happy.

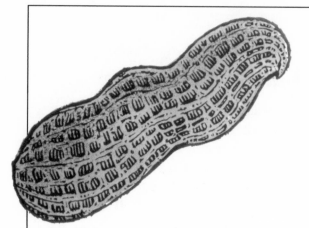

BOILED PEANUT
September 24 through October 23

You have a passionate desire to help your fellow man. Unfortunately, those who know you best—your friends and loved ones—may find that your personality is much too salty, and their criticism will probably affect you deeply because you are really much softer than you appear.

You should go right ahead and marry anybody you want to because, in a certain way, yours is a charmed life. On the road of life you can be sure that people will always pull over and stop for you.

BUTTER BEAN
October 24 through November 22

Always invite a Butter Bean because Butter Beans get along well with everybody. You, as a Butter Bean, should be proud. You've grown on the vine of life and you feel at home no matter what the setting. You can sit next to anybody.

However, you too shouldn't have anything to do with Moon Pies.

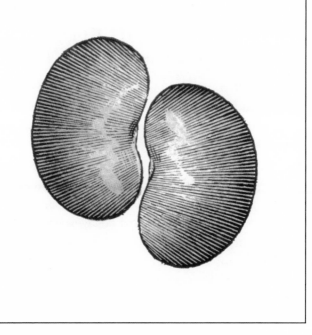

61

ARMADILLO

November 23 through December 21

You have a tendency to develop a tough exterior, but you are actually quite gentle. A good evening for you? Old friends. A fire. Some roots, fruit, worms and insects.

You are a throwback. You're not concerned with today's fashions and trends. You're not concerned with *anything* about today. You're really almost pre-historic in your interests and behavior patterns.

You probably want to marry another Armadillo, but Possum is another, somewhat kinky, mating possibility.

OKRA

December 22 through January 20

Although you appear crude, you are actually very slick on the inside.

Okras have tremendous influence. An older Okra can look back over his life and see the seeds of his influence everywhere.

Stay away from Moon Pies.

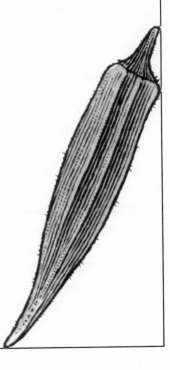

CHITLIN
January 21 through February 19

Chitlins often come from humble backgrounds. Many times they are uncomfortable talking about just where they came from. A Chitlin, however, can make something out of himself if he's motivated and has plenty of seasoning.

When it comes to dealing with Chitlins, be very careful. Chitlins can burn and then erupt like Vesuvius, and this can make for a really terrible mess.

Chitlins are best with Catfish and Okra. Remember that when marriage time rolls around.

BOLL WEEVIL
February 20 through March 20

You are beset by an overwhelming curiosity. You're unsatisfied with the surface of things, and you feel the need to bore deep into the interior of everything. Needless to say, you are very intense and driven, as if you had some inner hunger.

Nobody in their right mind is going to marry you, so don't worry about it.

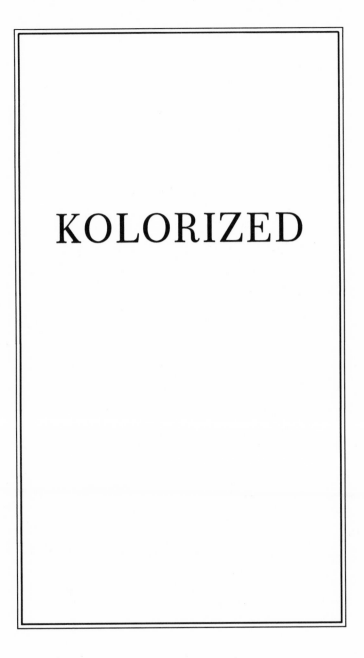

KOLORIZED

I own them. I can do what I want with them.

IT WAS IN THE AFTERNOON when K arrived. It was a small nondescript town, but K knew that in the town there was what he was seeking: the castle.

The castle hill was hidden, veiled in mist and darkness. On the wooden bridge leading from the main road to the village, K stood for a long time gazing into illusory emptiness above him. He could just barely make out the lime green, blinking neon light that said CASTLE, CASTLE, CASTLE. Underneath the sign he could see a red glowing VACANCY sign, but he could not tell if the little NO sign was on or not.

Then he went on to find quarters for the night. The inn was still awake, and although the landlord was upset by such a late and unexpected arrival, he was willing to let K sleep in a room in the back with Monte Carlo mint walls and grape sherbet carpeting. K was disappointed. He had been thinking about something in a pale goldenrod with topaz bordering, but he accepted it.

K went to his room. He threw back both the sea green, zebra-patterned cover spread on the bed and the fiesta cranberry sheet underneath. Then he changed into a lay-

69

ered fuchsia kangaroo top and some purple drawstring sweatpants and swiftly fell into a deep sleep.

But very shortly he was awakened. A young man was standing beside him along with the landlord. The young man had a Mediterranean skin tone and blue-violet eyes that were set off by his brick-red shirt with coral buttons, which he wore over a pair of cinnamon slacks. All of this was set off by what he wore on his feet: a pair of moonbeam melon slip-ons. The landlord was wearing an aqua mist shirt over a pair of spice brown pleated slacks.

The young man apologized very courteously for having awakened K, and then said: "This village belongs to the castle, and whoever lives here or passes the night here does so, in a manner of speaking, in the castle itself. Nobody may do that without the count's permission. But you have no such permit, and they would never give a permit to anybody who wears fuchsia with purple."

K half-raised himself, trying to keep the fuchsia top hidden under the sea green zebra-patterened cover spread.

"Who do I get a permit from?" he asked.

"The count," said the young man. "He is the only one able to give permits, but if you show up dressed like that, you might as well forget it."

K thanked the young man. He got out of bed and changed into a green heather leisure suit with autumn wheat trim. He prepared to go out looking for the castle.

"Before you go," said the young man, "I have two things I want to tell you. First, change those argyle socks. I've got some jungle grass ones I'll let you borrow."

"Thanks," said K. "What's the other thing you want to tell me?"

"A little story, a parable, if you will."

"Go right ahead," said K. "I'll change socks while I listen."

In a calm voice, the young man began his story.

"Before the law stands a doorkeeper. He's got on an orange windbreaker over a sea island blue shirt and he's wearing light brown trousers. A man from the country comes up to the doorkeeper and asks for admittance to the law. The doorkeeper looks at the man from the country, who is wearing a black and red mock turtle neck with drop shoulders and a pair of yellow pleated Bermuda shorts. The doorkeeper says that he cannot grant admittance at the moment. At first the man from the country thinks that it's all over, but then he asks if he might be allowed in later.

" 'It's possible,' says the doorkeeper, 'if you go home and change.'

"So the man from the country went home, and when he got back he was wearing a green spread-collar shirt with bold yellow stripping and a red polka-dot tie. And the gatekeeper took one look, burst out laughing and shut the gate.

"Forever."

K went out to look for the castle. He talked to many people who claimed to have been in the castle. He talked to many people dressed in many different shades: federal indigo, royal amethyst, deep strawberry, light pumpkin.

Still, he got no closer to the castle. Finally, exhausted, K changed into a Parisian violet sleep shirt and fell asleep.

K had a very vivid dream. In the dream he saw the castle. It was all black and white—really gloomy! It was depressing in there. Everything was either gray or black. It looked like the bottom of an ashtray or something. Just really depressing. Like one of the men's rooms at Fenway.

Then he saw a man. He was a man with a skinny mustache. This man had a little cup with him, and he kept spitting into it. This man reached into his pocket and he took something out. K could not tell what it was at first, but after a while K realized that it was big bucks. The man had big bucks in his hand.

Suddenly everything was different, and it was so much nicer. K especially enjoyed the castle's light chocolate valances, its federal blue wall-to-wall carpeting and, more than anything else, its cozy red cotton upholstery, everywhere!

It was a dream castle. Now.

BRET, LIKE, BRAINSTORMS

BRET'S EDITOR: Good to see you again. Here, have a beer and tell me what you've been up to.

BRET: Okay, it's like I've just really used up the I'm-eighteen-years-old-and-I'm-totally-ill thing, and I'm thinking, well that's all there is, the I'm-eighteen-years-old-and-I'm-totally-ill. And I already did that. I can't do that again. I might as well go to Betty Ford. I need to write things. Which is why we're just sitting here in these chairs in this room and I can't understand why we're doing this. Because it seems like too much trouble and maybe we should just go to the spa or something because I always go on Tuesdays and Thursdays and I'm thinking about all this and we're sitting here.

BRET'S EDITOR: Tell me about your new book, why don't you do that? Relax. Sort of fill me in. Are you okay?

BRET: Yeah.

BRET'S EDITOR: Are you really tense?

BRET: Yeah.

BRET'S EDITOR: Good. You want a lude, something?

BRET: "No," I hear myself say.

BRET'S EDITOR: Now you're cooking.

BRET: So I start talking and everything starts coming back

to me about what you're saying, because you said that word "book" and it reminded me of some of Shriekback's lyrics, "Book book. A book book." And I connected to that until it was playing over and over and over and over and you don't even have any records. And this whole office reminds me of someplace where my father goes and suddenly I realize that you remind me of some guy that I met outside Steak 'n' Brew and he was a black dude with a "Surrender Dorothy" T-shirt and I start to think.

BRET'S EDITOR: Please go on. I'm with you.

BRET: I'm sitting here in this Eames chair . . .

BRET'S EDITOR: It's not an Eames. It's a La-Z-Boy recliner.

BRET: So you just stop me right in the middle of what I'm saying and say something else and I scratch the side of my face and then we don't say anything for a while.

BRET'S EDITOR: Sorry.

BRET: It doesn't matter.

BRET'S EDITOR: I know.

BRET: So I'm sitting here in this office that reminds me of my dad's office where he slapped me around and then gave me a big stack of twenties to be quiet. And I look over and see you and I see that you're wearing a tweed suit from Macy's and some Docksides and you're asking me questions and I'm really nervous because I don't have any other life except the life when I'm eighteen.

BRET'S EDITOR: You've paused here, and I feel that I should say something to get you to talk again.

BRET: And I flash on a lot of scenes, coming back to my house from Betty Ford and I'm in the back seat and I am nodding and the people I'm with just pick up my carrier and bring me inside and I sleep with both of them at the same time and I remember looking over at dad and seeing him, naked, with his eyes closed and really tanned and Mommy next to him naked with her head turned under her elbow because I was taking up way too much of the bed but they both looked really nice with their perfect tans and I was over on the side in my pajamas with the feet, with a perfect tan, lying on my back screaming.

BRET'S EDITOR: Let me just say that this sounds like a novel.

BRET: Then I'm sitting on the dhurrie, leaning back on my elbows, looking at the tree blink on and off, and I'm thinking that there is no way that I'm going to get what I'm after unless I go out and get what I want for Christmas. Unless I go out and get some phony IDs and try to bluff my way up to the front of the line at the mall. When I get up there I find myself just throwing up all over Santa Claus and they take me outside and I lie down and I start to feel a little better but then some security guard comes over and asks me how I feel and I tell him "I don't know."

BRET'S EDITOR: This is very good stuff. The "A" stuff.

BRET: And then it's recess and I walk into the boys' room and it's empty and I stand there and look at myself and it's very quiet in there, almost like a tomb, but you can hear drifting in through the window, "Honey. Sugar sugar. You are my candy, girl. And you got me goin'." Then I just find myself crying and laughing until I almost pass out because I don't have any candy and I just ate my last little wax bottle almost an hour ago and I don't have any money for licorice.

BRET'S EDITOR: This has been wonderful and I have to say that your fears about running out of material seem a little strange, to say the least. It sounds to me like you have maybe three or four more books' worth of material, just based on what I've just heard.

BRET: I gotta go.

BRET'S EDITOR: Take care then. See you soon. You're not driving are you?

BRET: No.

BRET'S EDITOR: Real good then. I'll talk to you soon.

BRET: I kill the beer that I've been drinking and then I go over to the little refrigerator that he has in his office. I open it and I see that he has quite a lot of beer in there. I grab a Heineken and stuff it down my Ginocchietti sweatshirt. Then I open a Beck's and walk out with the Heineken cold right next to my skin.

BRET'S EDITOR: Take care.

DUCK!

WHEN YOU START IN TALKING about ducks and the South's obsession with these things, a good place to start is Shogun Japan. In *Shogun*, Blackthorne, the English guy, does something right for a change and all the Japanese guys want to reward him. They offer him a geisha girl, but Blackthorne, being English, doesn't go in for any of that. Bewildered by the English guy's reaction, the Japanese guys ask him if he wants a boy. Blackthorne is really appalled at this. One Japanese guy in the back says, "Maybe he wants a duck."

In the South we want, it seems, ducks.

I, for one, have never paid that much attention to ducks. I knew they were out there, but I never noticed them. Sometimes I'd go to the park and check out the ducks they had there. Suddenly, I began to see ducks *inside*.

I went over to a friend's house and his whole house was duck. There was a great deal of duck lamps, duck photos, and duck ashtrays. There was duck wallpaper in the bathroom, and once I got finished in there, I had to come out and see duck place mats.

Thank God we had chicken for dinner, but there were many ducks in there. Ducks in drawers. Ducks under glasses. Ducks everywhere. The phone rang and my friend went over and picked up this duck and started talking into it.

I was deeply disturbed: what was going on here?

I talked to Linda Parish Titus, an interior designer with J. T. Interiors, one of the biggest interior design companies in the South.

"Are ducks still big?" I asked.

I might as well have asked if Godzilla was still big. Ducks are very big. On the day we talked Ms. Titus was working on three separate duck-related jobs. These involved duck draperies, duck wallpaper and duck valences. I didn't know what a valance was, so I didn't ask her about it, but she sees no end to this duck thing.

How did it get here? No one knows for sure, but according to Ms. Titus the fault here lies, like most things, with men. In the pre-duck days, it seems that there was only one "masculine" pattern: some kind of plaid. Ducks were around of course, but since men never did any decorating, or had any *input*, as they say, the only place you saw ducks was on Father's Day cards. Then, as men started to actually *notice* what was around them, they decided to remake their world in their own image, and it was now duck time.

"It started with borders," said Ms. Titus.

Has the duck thing peaked?

Maybe.

Three months ago you'd hear "Oh, what a cute idea, ducks!" Now, says Ms. Titus, you often hear "Why are there all these ducks?"

But what if it doesn't go away? They said that rock 'n' roll was going to go away, but, as we all know, rock 'n' roll is here to stay. What will the future be like?

Cosmopolitan, August 1997

I WAS MARRIED TO A DUCK PERSON

We were both free-lance writers and we would go to the same parties and we would say hello and talk for a moment and we knew each other's names and then we started to sleep together but then I found out that he was a duck person.

I remember waking up very early one Sunday and seeing his suspenders with the ducks, all bunched up on the bureau where I told him never to throw things.

And I remember just sitting up and sobbing while I watched a couple videos.

STANDARD
LOATHSOME
THINGS

WHAT IS IT WITH US (the human race) and bugs? We just don't seem to like each other, do we? It's rare when you'll see someone, say a big pretty blond girl, sit on the sofa, cross her big pretty legs, look you right in the eye and say, "Bugs? I'm crazy about them."

This has happened to me, but I seriously doubt that it's going to happen to you. The big blond girl was an entomology major who went off to devote her life to the study of bugs, leaving me to become the shattered, twisted hulk of humanity that I now am.

> Her? She's actin' happy
> Lookin' at her bugs
> And me, I'm ridin' in my taxi
> Takin tips
> And meetin' slugs.

Let us now set aside prejudices and preconceptions. Let us look at a bug as the thing it is. Let us examine the phenomenon and forget, for a moment, that the phenomenon is really just gicky with all those arms and wriggly and sickening.

That should be easy to do.

• • •

A lot of people hate bugs. They hate the way they look. They hate the way they act. Especially, they hate the way they feel. Who hasn't dreamt of thousands of insects crawling all over your body? Maybe not your body, but somebody's body. I've never had any dreams like that, but I bet that most people have, just from asking around.

When I was a kid, I would go with my dad to the little working-man's bar that he ran, and he would, early in the morning, spread something called J. O. Paste on Ritz crackers and put them on the baseboard around the inside of the bar. This was for roaches, but the extraordinary thing was the J. O. Paste. When you opened a can of J. O. Paste, actual smoke came out. The smoke would continue to come out as my father spread this stuff on the Ritz crackers. Then he would put the spread crackers down on the baseboard and replace the top of the J. O. Paste jar and put the jar on a shelf in the back room. Sometimes, when he finished, he'd point to the jar of J. O. Paste and say, "Stay away from that."

I guess so.

For a while there, when I was a kid, they used to make very cheap "terror" movies merely by showing close-ups of insects and juxtaposing them with terrified people like starlets and Marshall Thompson. *Them* was about giant grasshoppers that get all over big buildings. You see a lot of terrified, screaming people looking through their windows at close-ups of grasshoppers. There was even a movie called *The Preying Mantis*. It was very bluntly named, but frightening. It was "found terror." You didn't even have to make up a title. All you had to do was call Marshall Thompson.

I have eaten bugs. Many of them. The first time was when I was in college, at the University of Georgia. I was at a party, and it was that in-between-time when you've been there for a while, but you don't really feel that you can say that you're leaving yet. There was something horrible playing—some Joni Mitchell vapor-girl stuff—so dancing was definitely out. I was in the kitchen. I saw a big roach scurry across the Formica. I picked it up and ate it. People looked at me like I was sick, but later I was able to dance with one of the women.

In Washington, D.C., in the natural history part of the Smithsonian, there is a strange little place on the second floor. It's a very nice little place, all neat and clean, and boys and girls go there all the time. When they get there they see a nice man come out, and he's smiling and being nice. And then you see that he has the most hideous giant insect crawling around on his forearm.

Sometimes it's a pretty standard loathsome thing, like a scorpion, crawling around on his forearm. Sometimes it's something esoteric, like a hissing cockroach from Madagascar. It's always something that almost makes you sick to look at, that much is pretty sure.

Once I walked in and the guy had a standard tarantula

on his forearm. A little kid asked him if it was poisonous, and the guy turned around, stared at the kid and said, "Deadly." He said it exactly like James Bond.

There was something vaguely familiar in the lilt of the voice.

The girl's voice became suddenly alert. "Is that insect there on your wrist poisonous?" she asked.

"Deadly," he answered.

"What name did you say?" Her eyes flashed. There was a pause.

"Bond," he said, "James Bond."

"I'm Moneypenny," she said.

"Dear old Moneypenny!"

They embraced warmly.

This never happened of course, but the guy does act like James Bond about the bug on his arm. Go see him at the Smithsonian when you're in the nation's capital.

Or maybe, just maybe, you should go downstairs, late at night, and have a good look at what's going on down there. Bring a flashlight, and wear shoes, but don't bring your American Express card. Because it's no good down there.

WATERMELON

WATERMELON. Nice and red and juicy. It's hot out, and the sun is going down. Sounds pretty good.

But, no. There's something wrong here.

Harry Markson, who used to be the publicist for Madison Square Garden, told a story about Joe Louis being given a watermelon to pose with for a publicity picture. This was right before his fight with Primo Carnera, a very big fight. Louis, it seems, *loved* watermelon. He ate it on a daily basis, whether he was training or not.

Louis, who was among the most amiable of men, wouldn't allow anybody to take his picture with a watermelon.

Reporters kept yelling, "Well, why not, Joe? Make a great shot, Joe, great shot."

"I don't like watermelon," said Louis.

And that, I guess, was that.

But what is the deal with this watermelon thing?

It requires a long growing season, that's for sure. So it seems pretty damn inevitable that we have a lot more of it than they have up North. Up North they also have watermelons, but the watermelons up there are a little bit on the laughable/pathetic side. For instance, one of the big

Northern varieties of watermelon is called (I'm not making this up, honest) *New Hampshire Midget.*

If that's not laughable/pathetic, I don't know what is.

In the South, we don't have laughable/pathetic. What we do have is creepy/guilty. Our big variety is called *Dixie Queen.*

Which is it going to be? Laughable/pathetic or creepy/guilty? Or yogurt, maybe?

Me, I'm going to get a big slice and sit under a tree and eat it. A big slice of *Dixie Queen.* Just don't take my picture.

VANNA
KARENINA

HAPPY, PERKY FACES are all the same. Unhappy, unperky faces are all different.

It was clear to Vanna as she looked at the contestants that they were a hideous, loathsome lot. There was nothing for anyone to be happy or perky about. Vanna thought about all these things and bubbled and smiled.

An accountant from Encino got "Free Spin." Vanna thought that it would be interesting to ask him just what he thought all this meant. Could it save him from his miserable life as an accountant in Encino? Did he actually think that? She stared at him and clapped as she had these thoughts.

Vanna thought to herself as she strode across the letter platform in a green flounce drop-shoulder gown by Mackie. She turned around and turned the lighted letter, which turned out to be an *R*.

R, she thought. *Why R we born?* She could not conceive of a position in which life would not be a misery. *We all must suffer,* she thought, *that is the condition of life, yet we never acknowledge that, we just go on living our futile lives. Yet, when one sees the truth, who is one to tell? What is one to do?*

97

Walk over to the puzzle platform and turn a letter around. And that is just what Vanna did.

She thought of the many people in her life: SER _ _ Y IV _ _ _ VITCH, KATA _ _ _ OV, KOZN _ _ _ EV. They had all meant so much before, when they had won the right to come back. Some of them had come back for an entire week! Now Vanna could feel nothing for them. They were just like other pathetic, hopeless human wretches, like so much patio furniture with large price tags.

Vanna had seen so many contestants: teachers, doctors, lawyers, housewives, hoe-down announcers, city cops. Vanna seemed to see all their history, and all the crannies of their souls, as it were turning a light on in their inner-most beings. She knew everything. She had seen every-thing that there was to see about humanity: how some would keep their extra money on account even though there was an attractive curio cabinet still available, how some would have the puzzle solved and yet continue to spin the wheel out of sheer naked human greed. Greed, mendacity, really bad taste in clothes, bad spelling, she had seen it all. She had looked deep into the bowels of evil, smiled broadly and bubbled.

She thought of the first day she had met VR _ _ SKY. How foolish she had been. How could she love a man who wouldn't even tell her all the letters in his name? She had been such a fool, but now she knew what she must do. It was as inevitable to her as the bonus round at the end of every show. She beamed a winning smile, clapped her hands together, walked off the letter platform and stood next to the wheel.

She stood motionless before the swiftly turning wheel. A feeling such as she had never known came over her. She crossed herself. Then she clapped her hands together and jumped up and down, squealing with excitement. Her life came flooding back to her. She saw her childhood. She was sitting over a steaming bowl of alphabet soup, lost in revery. She was standing in front of a full-length mirror at Gramps's house, practicing being perky. She had so many thoughts, so many memories.

Yet she did not take her eyes off the turning wheel. Suddenly she dove, face forward onto the wheel, impaling herself between "Lose a Turn" and "$450." As she felt her life ebb out, a life filled with so many troubles, so many falsehoods, so much sorrow, so much evil, so many of the glitziest gowns this side of dream date Barbie, she lifted her head, looked straight into the camera, smiled and waved "Bye-bye."

I'M THE MINIMALIST AROUND HERE

I'M WELL KNOWN around here. Down the street there's a fellow with a small engine shop who plays in a bluegrass band, and he's well known too. Up the street there's a lady who retired after teaching English to everybody for about forty years. She's well known. Still, I'm probably the most well known.

When people are visiting my town, they'll drive down the streets, and the people who they're visiting will tell them who lives where. They'll say that that guy owns a lumber yard and that guy works at a chicken plant and that guy is retired. But when they're driving by my house I know what they're saying. They're saying, "That guy that lives in that house, he's a minimalist."

And they're right. I'm the minimalist around here.

I've pared everything down until there's almost nothing left. When you talk to me you may think that I should just "loosen up," but then you'd be missing the whole point. When you're looking at me you're looking at minimalist, pure and simple. I'm as spare and lean as my prose.

Ask me what I did last night.

I bring Luther to Bobby Jean's party and Luther is wearing a Cat diesel hat and a T-shirt that says something, but you can't make it out because Luther is sweating too much. He's also got on a Lorus watch that he wears because he's got a really embarrassing tattoo on his wrist that he wants to hide. I went with him when he went to get the tattoo and it made me very tense.

We walk into Cooper's and I see all of these people I know: John, Edgar, Andrew, and twelve guys named "Bubbah." They're all standing around in front of this twinkly light thing they have at Coopers that makes it look like it's a waterfall.

"Hey," Bubbah says.

"Hey, Bubbah," I say.

I go over and get Shorty. We drive out to the lake and go frog-giggin'.

And I noticed that Shorty's arms were more tanned than mine.

"What's with the arms?" I ask.

Shorty says nothing.

I drive back to Cooper's and there's this song on the radio, "I'm Going to Get a WINO to Decorate Our House," and the words keep on in my brain and I'm really tense and I try to smoke a cigarette but I realize at the last second that I don't have any cigarettes because I don't smoke.

And I'm listening to this song and there's this line in it that just keeps saying "Baby's got her blue jeans on" and I am getting very tense standing around in there. So I decide that I will go stand someplace else so I move about three feet to my left and I try standing there for a while.

I go into the bathroom and I can see that they have these little prophylactic vending machines in there. I look at one and it says EXCITEMENT in big letters. Someone comes in and it's Luther.

"Busiest place in town," he says.

I don't say anything. I leave.

I walk out and see that J.B. is here now and he's talking to Bubbah.

I see that I'm standing next to this guy who just came in. He's wearing a "Bomber's Lures" hat.

"Where's Bubbah?" I say.

"Right there," he says.

"Not that Bubbah."

"Which Bubbah?"

"Another Bubbah."

"Does he look like that Bubbah?" He points at a guy named Bubbah.

"Yes," I say.

"Haven't seen him."

I don't say anything.

And right away I see this guy Bubbah, that I know, and he's leaning up against a cigarette machine and he's got just incredibly dirty hair. And I can see this other guy, Bubbah's mother; and she's playing pool with her son, Bubbah, who I know, and it looks like Bubbah is down at least three balls in eight-ball and I just feel that I have to leave and I say that.

I go over to get Shorty, who is talking to all of these people that I don't know. I think I may have met one of them at Bubbah's last year, but I'm not sure so I don't say anything.

"Shorty," I say.

"Yeah," he says.

"You about ready?"

"Yeah. Just let me finish this."

"Take it with you."

"OK," he says, "let's roll."

We walk toward the door. Suddenly I stop.

"Wait a second," I say.

"What?"

"Let me get one."

"Go ahead."

We drove back in silence and it was dark and we didn't even have the radio on.

There's this brief moment that's like a flash in my mind. I can't even tell you if it really happened or not. I went over to the pool table with two quarters and I look down and I see, like a million quarters, all lined up. And I'm standing there, with these two quarters, and I hear, "Hey, Bubbah."

So, can I kind of end here?

THE
TRIAL OF
ALLAN
BLOOM

So WE FINALLY GOT HIM out there. We had to cancel sixth period, but that was nothing because for most people, it was gym. So we get him out there, and we start talking to him, and he is just the biggest wienie in the world.

Jason asks him "what happened with your hair?" and everybody just cracked up.

Allan Bloom started mumbling about something and we all just got sick because we thought he might start "alluding" to something or get like that.

So Shane gets up and starts going on about how Allan Bloom likes to make everybody feel stupid. Like, what's his problem? And that wienie just sits there with a stupid expression on his face, like "I'm smarter than you are, so there." What a dweeb.

Then Bloom gets up to say something.

"Today there's no distinction between intellectuals and nonintellectuals . . ."

That's how he starts, I swear to God. Oh, maaaaaaaaaaaaaaan, I wish I had brought my Walkman.

Then he says that if George Washington was sitting here next to Mick Jagger, everybody would be interested in

Mick Jagger and nobody would want to talk to George Washington.

Jagger? Mick Jagger? George Washington? Who *are* these people? Is this guy from the moon, or what? Why would anybody want to talk to either of these people? Who cares?

Why does this rejamoe have to go on like this?

Then he starts really getting into it. He says that the teachers aren't the problem. The kids aren't the problem. We all know what the problem is. *He's* the problem. If he would just shut up we could all go home, go to wrestling practice, whatever.

But, *will* he shut up? Doubt it. Doubt it very much, thank you.

"We don't think anything is more important than anything else. That's our problem. We think everything's the same. We're all afraid to assign values to anything. We're afraid to say that Beethoven is perhaps better than Twisted Sister."

I was lost, for a second. All I could think of was my car sitting in the parking lot. But a wall-banger group behind me started talking.

"Sister, man," somebody said.

Bloom looked at them and they shut up in a hurry: Todd raised his hand. Bloom gave him a little nod. Todd got up. "Hey, as far as I'm concerned, I'm happy you came here. We all are. Everybody is really happy that you came here. And I'd like to say, as president of the student council, that the whole student body understands your concern about what we're learning here."

110

Everybody understood that that was Todd's way of saying that he recognized an old-guy-in-the-eighties/professor-guy-in-the-sixties thing.

Now, let's book.

But, no. We have to have more. We need more. Sure. Let's run over until the buses leave.

"I was just like you are, a natual American barbarian. But I managed to get a much deeper perspective on life because I somehow dug into certain books that are essential to our culture, to any culture."

Now, we book.

On the way out everybody starts making noises like cows, "Moooo, moooo." What a goof.

Jason yells up at Bloom, "Good-bye, Perfesser, sorry about the closing of your American Mama."

What a trip.

Mooooooo!

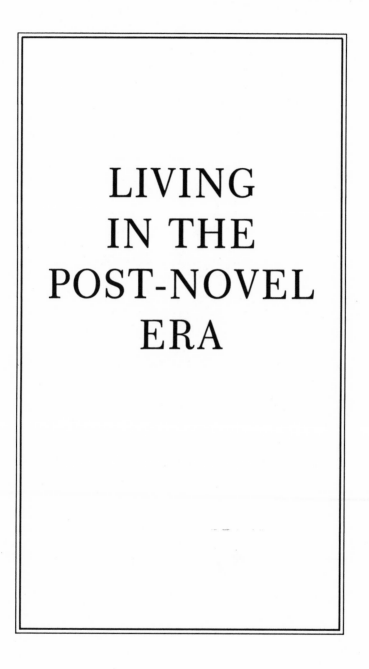

LIVING
IN THE
POST-NOVEL
ERA

In individual or collective manifestoes, the most oddly assorted literary types have announced to their startled colleagues that it's no longer possible to tell stories; that the hero no longer serves as the focus of the action; that plot, character and psychology belong in the dustbin of history; that writing should cease altogether.

—PETER SCHNEIDER
The New York Times Book Review

I'M REALLY A GREAT WRITER but, given the particular age in literature I was born in, I've had to channel my energies into unusual forms of writing. There was no need for, say, a great novel anymore. The end of the novel came when Norman Mailer called Truman Capote "a ballsy little guy." If our novelists are talking like that, why bother?

For a while there I concentrated on "cheery little notes." I worked in that particular form for a number of years, but I finally abandoned it after I wrote:

> Have a good time in Seattle! Don't
> do anything I wouldn't do!

Putting down my pen, after writing the last word of that cheery note, I knew, somehow, that I would never write another cheery note. I had pushed the form to its limits, and now it was time to explore other modes of written expression. My web was finished; I started another web.

For a long time I didn't write anything. My nights were sleepless and my days were almost sleepless too. I found myself drinking too much, talking to strangers, waking up in strange beds, scratching myself too much. I tried to tell myself that this was a normal stage in my evolution as a writer and that it would probably be over soon and I would find myself writing better than ever, but in a new, untried form.

August 3, 1987. A mundane day for most people, but for me it marked a new beginning. It was on that day, at 9 A.M., that I wrote my first letter to Blue Cross/Blue Shield complaining about a mistake in their billing records.

These letters have, of course become familiar to almost everybody who reads, and are, I guess you might say, classics of the genre. Let me just touch on the highlights.

8/17/87 Could you please at least *check* your records again on the *remote* possibility that one of you fine folks down there made a completely unintentional blunder?

8/24/87 I am sending along a *copy* of my canceled check. I'm not, as you suggest, sending along the actual check, because I have a hard time believing that one of you idiots won't lose *this* check too.

8/31/87 Do you cheat everybody?

9/3/87 Don't you even *try* to earn your salary?

This was a fertile period for me. It was as if my writing muse, so long dormant, was now really heavily into aerobics. I thought at one time that I could go on writing letters to Blue Cross/Blue Shield forever. However, however sadly, that period in my writing ended too. At this time in my career I seemed to be restless, aware of the ticking clock. Above all else I needed to move on.

For a long time—maybe six or seven weeks—nothing. I just couldn't keep my fingers on the typewriter. There was always something stopping me: a phone call, an appointment, the police. Then, just like before, a little cloud lifted and I could see the direction that my writing should go.

It was headed right for Walter Scot. Not Walter Scott, that old Scotsman. He was a novelist and I knew that the novel road had ended with a steel-reinforced brick wall. I wasn't stupid. No, my Walter Scot (who, if you notice, spells his name different from Mr. Ivanhoe) doesn't hang around in medieval land; my Mr. Scot hangs around in the front of *Parade* magazine, and he marches in a little thing they call "Walter Scot's Personality Parade."

It was there that I found my new direction.

Q: How old is Ted Koppel? Does he dye his hair? Is he AC/DC?

With "Personality Parade" I found that I was writing as well as ever. Maybe better.

Q: Who is older, Morgan Fairchild or Bryant Gumbel? Is it true that neither one is allowed into Nebraska? Are they AC/DC?

I felt animated with the very spirit of creativity during this period. Perhaps, for the first time in my long writing career, I felt that I was creating a body of work which might never grow tedious, writing that would express a wild yet tender sensitivity, yet at the same time a writing that would evoke images of a hard, tough man sitting at his desk and typing.

Q: Is it true that James Michener's recent best-seller *Legacy* was inspired by Bruce Willis's recent HBO special, "The Return of Bruno"? Also, are you AC/DC?

I had never written better. Perhaps that's why I had to stop. Perhaps I was intimidated by my own achievement. Maybe it was just time for a rest, pure and simple. It was the late nineteen nineties.

For a while, perhaps ten years or so, I abandoned the written word altogether and reverted to the oral tradition of my ancestors. Whenever I went to a bar to hear the tunes, I'd always sit way in the back of the room, as far away from the band as I could. I'd sit very quietly for a long time, but then, at eleven-thirty, when there was a little pause, I'd request that the band play "Whiskey and Women."

In a sense, this satisfied me. Even though I wasn't writing, I was expressing my nature and fulfilling my creative needs. Yet it was never quite enough. I grew tired of it. Eventually I started requesting "This Diamond Ring" by Garry Lewis and the Playboys. Soon, I stopped even that.

Yet I was still eager to explore the possibilities of the oral form. I went to a party where I didn't know anybody, stood next to the aquarium and talked about the fish. When I walked out of that house on that evening I knew one thing: whatever else life may confront me with I know one thing: never again will I go back to the oral tradition. I knew that one thing.

My friends that I met while standing next to the aquarium were almost all disappointed. Yet my mind was made up; my work could not ever be oral. It was just not intended. My work would be in the written form. My work, such as it was, would be for Walter Scot's "Personality Parade."

And thus I returned, never regretting a single moment.

All important literary careers follow an arc. Just like the year, the lives of writers have seasons. I spent twenty years writing questions to "Personality Parade." I wouldn't have known that it was that long if a young friend hadn't pointed it out to me.

Now I can finally pause and look back over my life as a writer. I can savor its peaks. I can, finally, almost even appreciate its valleys.

My life as a writer has brought me many things: vivid reminders, quiet pleasures, sunlit walks along exotic shores, the girls, the paint, the Porsche. All of this I had. Because I was a writer. But I didn't write any novels.

FURTHER
IRONIES
OF THE
BIG CHILL
GENERATION

By NOW WE'VE SEEN a lot of people who, when they were nineteen, smeared their bodies with war paint and ran naked onto a big field to protest something. We are no longer surprised when we hear that that same person now drives a station wagon, takes the kids to school when it's raining and lives in the suburbs. We're all used to that. We've heard all those stories. We've seen how somebody who tied up the dean of his college can later become a member of the Presbyterian church council. We're all a little tired of that.

When somebody tells you something like *that*, you don't feel like saying "That's *ironic*" anymore. You might change the subject, but if you're like most of us you just put your head down and wait.

I remember that in the sixties I had long hair and sideburns. I remember getting into heated discussions about what album covers meant and all that.

Yet today, I have a 1986 Toyota and I've been married for ten years and have three children.

The biting irony of that somehow gnaws at my nervous system. Was I alone? I thought, just as I suspected, alienated? Might there not be someone, somewhere, who shared my experiences? Someone else who had the same sort of unpleasant feeling from having something ironic about them?

I thought so.

EDWARD J. "PARTY" HOFFLAND, 37

I always used to think and read about the "British Invasion" and, I guess, I was "wild" then.

Today, first of all, I'd like to take this opportunity to thank everybody in this shop for all the nice things you've done for us the past week. We always look forward to coming out here each year because we know that we'll never be treated better by anybody, anyplace.

And I also have to say that things look good; they look good for all of us and we have every reason to believe that next year will be even better than this year.

I'm sorry about how I mentioned that I liked the "British Invasion," but I feel good standing here in front of everybody and admitting that.

And, just in closing, the answer is "No, I haven't hired a motorcycle gang to serve as bodyguards. I'm not a 'kook.' "

Thank you.

MARK STARK, 38

I've always felt that a revolutionary is, first and foremost, a doomed man. I've always felt that, and I still do feel that.

I've always felt that unless you were willing to face death, you had no business calling yourself a revolutionary, and might as well just stop all the pretense of being a revolutionary at all. You might as well get yourself a blue suit and sell cars for a living.

Today, as I was talking to this fat guy about a Plymouth Sundance, I began to think about the way everything once was. It "blew my mind" for a second there, but I was finally able to make the sale and send that slob off to the business office to sign the papers. I watched that guy walk away and I'm telling you, that guy was a *pig*. He needed to *drop* a few.

I think it was the rust-proofing protection thing that made it a go.

Bobby "Boogaloo" Watts, 39

Once I really enjoyed sitting and listening to

> Straight collar, conservative flashing down the street
> What are you sayin' to whoever you meet?
> You'll never tame me
> You'll never know
> The things
> That I know
> You'll never do the things that I do
> You will never be the way that I am
> Let me be free
> To be the way that I am

That's never really come in that handy with clients.

Kenny "Rock and Roll" Kondritzer, 36

Yeah I had that job, but it was just a summer thing while I was going to school. The summer before I had been a groundskeeper, but they didn't need me that particular summer. That's what they told me anyway. It was probably because I had to punch out Kevin Fallon, whose dad owned the stupid cemetery, one night in the Ratskeller because he was trying to put the moves on Trina Cooper, who I of course had a thing for and was with.

Then Fallon's old man finds out and all of a sudden I can't mow lawns in his goddamn cemetery anymore and I was counting on that for my summer employment.

Anyway, that's why I have "Urban Guerrilla" there on my résumé. It was just a summer thing.

Elaine "Bitsy" Mezger, "Over Thirty, I Guess. Say That."

At one time, I am quite sure, I was branded as an enemy of the government of the United States. I had no problem with that because there were so many countries that would harbor me, and I felt secure about the revolution and my role in it. I felt very sure that ultimately the power structure and all the racist pigs would be ousted and the revolution would take place.

Today, I'm still busy, still working. This morning I spent studying "the microwave gourmet" and working on a few things. I think I can say now that the microwave oven is much more than a time-saving device. You can really use it to prepare some of the most delicious dishes that you've ever tasted. Soon more and more people will begin to think this way. I'm convinced that no matter how much they surpress this, we're going to see more and more cooking big meals with the microwave. This is the future.

They will capture universities. They will march in demonstrations. They will fight police. They will appear in newspapers and on television, waving the flags of radicalism.

One day we will all cook really big meals—three or four courses—in microwave ovens.

And then, maybe then, we can all start to get into making afghans.

Harold Parish, 37, Once Known as "Sensitive"

I remember all this like it was yesterday. You were reading that book, Emily Dickinson, I think, or something, and I was sitting across from you and I was reading some Robert Frost, and I remember you leaning over and asking me if you could borrow one of my bookmarkers, and I remember getting very upset and asking you why you couldn't get your own bookmarkers, and I remember you making some kind of sarcastic remark, and I remember just sitting there until the shadows came and washed the room.

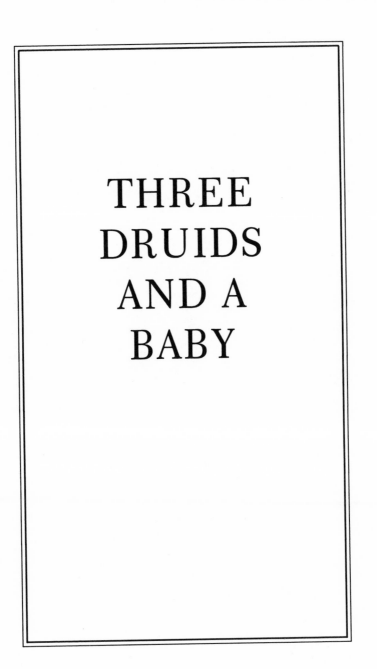

THREE
DRUIDS
AND A
BABY

I HAD JUST COME HOME from work. I was exhausted. I had just spent nine hectic hours building a giant wickerwood goat. It had been just murder, but finally it was over. Tomorrow, when we put the victims inside and set it on fire, I would know that it had all been worthwhile. Now I looked forward to a hot meal and a nice relaxing evening at home in the bachelor pad I shared with Baille-shan and Tor-Aillinn, two Druid pals.

The first thing I thought when I walked into my living room was *Something is wrong here.* I turned around and then I saw it. Somebody had put a *baby* in here! What are three hard-working single Druids doing with a baby?

When Baille-shan and Tor-Aillinn got home they were just about as stunned as I was. We didn't know what to do, so we slaughtered a ferret and looked at his entrails. We decided that we would try to do the best that we could.

That night the three of us sat around and boiled a cow's flesh in a pot. Then we all got in the pot and took a bath. We brought the baby in with us because we wanted everything to be as normal as possible. Then we got out and curled up and went to sleep. And while we slept we had a vision of the future king of Tara, but then the baby peed all over everything.

We were all in our thirties. We had been bachelor Druids for a long, long time. By now we had so many quirks that we couldn't get a *woman*, much less a baby, to live with us. We didn't commit our learning to writing so there were never any "Reminders."

It seemed chaotic, but we, as Druids, had to do it this way. We got used to it. After a while any woman or child would, too.

We dyed ourselves blue and we wore goat head pieces.

We were set-in-our-ways bachelors.

But we weren't bad guys.

"Let's hire a nurse," suggested Tor-Aillinn. We all said no to that. If three Druids couldn't raise a baby, who could?

We all decided that we were of one mind about this. We pitched in. We all helped out. We moved our schedules around to accommodate the baby.

Soon, though, we were ready to give that baby an urn burial. We decided, in a good-natured way, to *not* do that. As we sat around the fire and discussed whether or not we should give the baby an urn burial, we all learned a lot about ourselves as we watched our faces in the firelight. Our decision also said a lot about the kind of Druids we were.

Good Druids.

Once, Tor-Aillinn was all alone with the baby, and he was having a very hard time. Then he told her the story of the

Druids who were planning to sacrifice slaves, but then the Druids found out that they didn't have enough slaves, so instead they sacrificed some relatives. At the end of the story that baby was out cold.

Trill-Illeen, our leader, was a very old man. It was obvious to us now that he wouldn't be around too much longer. Although we did not often speak about it, we all knew that soon Trill-Illeen would go on to his next life, and we would be left without a leader. It was traditional among us Druids to vote on a new leader in such situations, but often there had been violent disagreement among the Druids at the death of a leader. There was often armed violence at the death of a leader. The death of a king brought many troubles. Baille-shan, Tor-Aillinn and I sat together in front of the fire. We all knew that with the death of Trill-Illeen we might find ourselves on opposite sides in some future power struggle. We might find ourselves on opposing sides in murderous combat. We might find ourselves in the position of having to kill a roommate without asking him about the damage deposit on the apartment.

Baille-shan, Tor-Aillinn and I sat silently in front of the fire, its glow dancing menacingly over our countenances. Is there any grimmer thought than the thought that you may have to kill your friend?

It would have really gotten depressing if the baby hadn't peed on us and lightened things up.

Later, on the sixth day of the moon, everybody was really frantic down at the office because there had been a hell of a lot of sacred mistletoe, and we were real short on help that year. It was absolutely the worst time in the world to have a baby, especially in a bachelor pad with two other Druids.

One night we were all very tired, but the baby started crying. We tried everything that night, the repertoire.

Tor-Aillinn made funny faces. Baille-shan killed a large animal and studied its entrails. I killed a slave. Yet she wouldn't stop crying. We were at our wits' end. Finally, she peed on us, and we all shared a little knowing laugh.

We were becoming better and better Druids.

VOICES
OF THE
FOOTBALL
STRIKE

YEAH, I remember it. It was after that Monday night game between the Jets and New England. I walked into the kitchen and sat down. I thought hard. In five days it would be Sunday. It was fall. Yet there would be no football games. I sat and I sat and I thought and I thought. I just couldn't picture it in my mind. This hole opened up in my life. On Sunday afternoon I would no longer know what to do.

Some guys lost it. You never knew how a guy was going to react. Even when you thought you knew the guy, things would just go nuts for some guys, and there was always a certain risk being around them. And these weren't guys from the moon or anything. These were guys that you *knew*. Guys you had sat around on the sofa and killed a twelve-pack with. Many twelve-packs.

Yet there was always that uncertainty, that little indecision. After a while, you could never lend a guy your shop-vac and be certain that you were ever going to see it again. You developed an attitude of no mercy about lending out any mechanical tools. Sure, I guess I became cynical.

You'd say I got cruel. Got hard. I'd just say that I was being realistic. The football strike did that to you.

At that time in my life I was younger than I am now, and I guess I could adapt to things pretty easy. People tell me I took it well, but how the hell do I know what "taking it well" is? I was just another guy. I never went for any of that John Wayne macho stuff then, and I still don't. It was just me and Sunday afternoon and no football. I just wanted to get on with things as best I could. Don't make a hero out of me.

A lot a people come up to me and act like I did something special. I tell them that a *lot* of guys remodeled their kitchens. A *lot* of guys installed garage door openers. A *lot* of guys installed finish flooring. I feel like saying, "For every guy like me, there were twenty guys who tried the same thing, but didn't make it. They're the ones you should be talking to. They're the ones who finally gave up and went back in and watched all those bartenders and forklift operators play football. Those are the people you should be thinking about. Those were the guys that meant something, guys who were faced with an absolutely hopeless situation, but wouldn't give up."

The Japanese have some word for that but I can't remember what it is.

One incident stands out in my mind. I was sitting on the floor in my living room doing a little weather-stripping. There was a knock on the door and I put down my hammer and went over and answered it. It was this little woman. She asked me if I wanted to join a letter-writing campaign about some damn thing. I don't know what came over me but I paused for a second, then I blindsided her.

As I was getting up from off her, I extended a hand and helped her up.

"Welcome to the NFL," I said, and I helped her brush some of the grass off her dress.

That's the way things were then. It wasn't like it is now.

I took some pictures of me during the football strike. I look at them and remember. I think, *That's me.*

It's hard to believe. But I have the photo there to remind me. It wasn't a video; it really happened.

I was always an athlete. I could do anything. I'd wash the car, take out the garbage, anything. I was always good at everything. But I never took it seriously. It came so easily to me that I guess I never thought of it as something that I might actually do as my life. Then the strike came and everything was different.

At first it was a big period of adjustment, but I think I finally settled into it. Then, just as I got used to taking out the garbage and washing the car on Sunday afternoon, it was all over. Just as suddenly as it had begun, it was gone. We all went back to being the way we were, just as if it had never happened at all.

You know, it's funny. I have a nephew who was born just after the football strike, and we're close, but there's that big difference between us. I was born on the other side of the football strike. Things that he can't imagine I know to be real. The football strike will just be a lot of fuzzy photographs and a history lesson in school to my nephew. I know different.

I was there.

THE FICTION
VERSION

FIRST TO ASSAULT the eye on the way down the aisle to the ring was a profusion of heads: some with hats on top of them, some black-haired, some gleaming in their baldness. Far down the aisle, the paradoxically square ring was a bright electric white, glowing ominously under the arc lights. Tyson remembered all of the rings he had seen in his life. There had been so many that they ran together and blurred in his memory. There was one thing that he remembered that they shared, one link that chained them together in his consciousness: all of the rings, every one, all of them, every single one, was square. Amid the confusion and the comings and goings and regrets and little heartaches, there was at least that: they were all square.

Beginning his slow, thoughtful way down to the ring, Tyson saw many faces, but one face made him stop walking and start thinking. It was a face staring at him from an aisle seat. There it was: a white face with white teeth clenched around a white cigarette, a white hat and a white shirt and yes, white shoes. Something clicked in Tyson's brain.

That guy is really white.

Leave that behind now. Don't we leave everything behind us?

Tyson was getting into the ring now. Three, four steps up. Rooney moved a strand of the rope to make it easier for him. How good a person Rooney was! But how cruelly he treated poor Rooney! Just last week Tyson had forgotten completely about Rooney's birthday! How contemptuous Tyson was of himself and what he had become. *Is this what I am?* he thought. *Is this what I do? Where am I? Who am I? What am I? Am I a "who" or a "what"?*

Sighing, Tyson got into the ring and started to bounce around. The crowd cheered loudly. He heard a hoarse voice yell, "Get this guy, Mike!" and another voice yell, "One round!" Then he heard another voice scream, "Stop being so damn introspective!"

Tyson allowed himself a fast look out at the crowd. It was a large, noisy crowd composed of all kinds of people. Tyson thought of the crowd, their quiet meaningless lives, their cars and their clothes, their cheap sordid little love affairs, their tiny hopes and dreams soon to be washed away in the great tide that is time.

He sighed again, and Rooney asked him to stop sighing so he could get the mouthpiece in.

Rooney rubbed his shoulders as Tyson walked over to the middle of the ring and stood motionless in front of Hosea, his "opponent." Such a cold word, Tyson thought. *Opponent.* How we seek to demean each other in the subtlest ways. As if that were all we were, opponents. But, in a way, wasn't it true? Weren't we all opponents for somebody? For some thing? Wasn't it really the truth? Wasn't that what was always waiting for us when we got out of bed and made coffee, just more and more opponents?

The ring announcer, a slick-haired fat man whose eyes couldn't hide the weariness within, took the microphone in one of his pudgy hands and began.

"In this corner, weighing two hundred and eighteen pounds . . ."

Suddenly Tyson froze. He knew that he was the one the announcer was talking about. His heart began to pump furiously. He could hardly catch his breath.

Liar, he thought. *Liar! Murderer! Skunk! Weasel! Vicious no-good stinker!*

Tyson knew that he had weighed in at two seventeen. He breathed deeply, almost out of control. *No*, he thought. *I won't say anything. I won't do anything. I'll just keep having these thoughts. Over and over. But why must these thoughts always end in a question? Why can't they ever end in a statement? Why always a question? Is there some deeper meaning behind the fact that they always end in a question? Is that just the way things are?*

Tyson had won. Surely he had won. Nothing else mattered. He felt a powerful sense of exhilaration in his spine. He allowed himself this moment of happiness before he started to have thoughts again.

Or would he?

I TURNED
IT AROUND

I TURNED IT AROUND. If anybody comes up to you and tells you that you can't, look him right in the eye and tell him, "No, you're wrong, I'm sorry to say. I read about this person in a magazine, and he quite successfully turned it around. So, you see, you're incorrect in saying that you can't turn it around. You're a very nice person and I'm very fond of you, but you *can* turn it around. I'm emphatic on that particular point."

I guess it started when I was very young. Very young. Just shockingly young. Someone told a friend of mine something during naptime and that "friend" told me. Then their friends told two other friends. Then their friends told their friends, and so on.

At first it was just fun. I looked at it as something that was available, appealing and harmless. I went along as if there wasn't anything wrong. By now I knew the ways of hiding things. I concealed. I hid. I deceived. I kept my head down, and kept right on whispering.

No one knew. I was good.

I kept on. I knew by now that I was strip-mining my soul, but what could I do?

I thought of various options, but I finally decided to keep on doing exactly what I had been doing. My life turned into a nightmare.

After a while I realized one thing: "Around here, I'm only getting two things, summer mud and winter snow."

But yet I kept on.

I remember once, I was heavily into everything wrong by then, I was coming back from recess and I saw four boys in my kindergarten class and, in my impulsive, on-the-edge way, I decided to join them. Somebody had some bread, and we passed it around and threw it to this squirrel. We got him so he was really close, he was almost eating out of our hands.

I remember thinking, *This is the greatest! My life has no meaning except for this!*

The bell rang. We were all late. We had to stay after and clap erasers. I didn't even care anymore. I was too far gone. I knew I was out of control, yet I refused to stop.

I became increasingly depressed and lost more weight. Time was running out. I kept getting in car accidents and my kidneys kept failing.

And all this time, I'm sad to say, I didn't even for one moment think of what I was doing.

It's all behind me now. I've turned it around.

How? one might ask.

Let me tell you.

Once a young intern walked into another hospital room. She was young and idealistic. She wore her hair in a bun and seemed aloof from the despair and pain that she found all around her. I remember her walking into my room. She took one step, then was pulled aside by another doctor who was already there. He was old and grizzled and grouchy. He took her by the arm and said, "Don't bother with that one. He's had it. It's a wash. Write him off."

He turned and walked out of the room. I was left alone with this idealistic young intern, but I had just moments earlier been written off by the best doctor in the state.

Just three weeks later I was back in business: buying big cars, closing big mortgages, driving away squatters.

Just kicking ass.

Eventually I even regained consciousness.

I look at it now as a long, slow crawl back, that period right after I got married to that intern, Doctor Paulette Piquet (just call her "Babe," I do. She's a hell of a woman and a great provider.)

Today I'm busy. Very busy. Doing some incredible things that are, more than likely, going to change the way we think of what it is to be human. My long-range goal is to completely alter human history, the earth and the life forms on earth.

I want to do that, *and* become a better person.

Who knows? Maybe I'll get lucky and make it. Maybe I won't. But even if it turns out I can't change human history, maybe I'll just be happy to sit on a beach and suck suds. Whatever happens will be great with me. I'm looking forward to tomorrow. I bought a telescope so I can see the exact moment when tomorrow begins and go nuts when it happens.

I'm up for it.

My doom was sealed but now I'm germinating. So don't let anybody tell you that you can't turn it around. You can. Because you read it in a magazine. And, after you turn it around, you can write a magazine article about it too.